S0-AGO-687

MOLE
MOVES HOUSE

WRITTEN BY
ELIZABETH BUCHANAN
ILLUSTRATED BY
GEORGE BUCHANAN

DOUBLEDAY
NEW YORK LONDON TORONTO SYDNEY AUCKLAND

When Mole first noticed Mr. Carrington at work in the garden, he knew at once that he had found a man after his own heart. Mr. Carrington was digging and he was doing a very good job.

Mole thought how proud he would be to work with such a good digger. He saw how much work there was to be done and imagined how delighted Mr. Carrington would be to have skilled help.

So Mole decided to move right away. He would become Mr. Carrington's neighbor.

On his first day as Mr. Carrington's new neighbor,
Mole helped to enlarge the vegetable patch. He could
tell that Mr. Carrington was surprised.

The next day Mole dug a new vegetable patch.
Mr. Carrington was amazed. That night Mr.
Carrington decided to do something for Mole.

Mr. Carrington worked all night long . . .

to finish the trap he was making.

When Mole woke up in the morning, it was his turn to be surprised. A fine new gate had been fitted over his biggest molehill!

Mole tucked his bootscraper into a convenient
position by the gate and set off in a hurry. One good
turn deserves another, and the herb garden was
definitely too small. Mole planned to do some fast
digging there!

As time went on, Mr. Carrington found more and more to do for Mole. He spent days designing a system to flood Mole's largest rooms with water. Then he set up a pump and a hose leading to Mole's 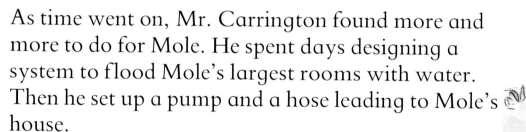 house.

Mole found some pipes and nozzles and set to work
with a mole wrench to do some plumbing. What a
luxury to have running water in his home!

In return for this kindness, Mole did a really good job excavating the flower bed.

Mr. Carrington went to a lot of trouble to discover
which wood burnt with the most choking black
smoke. He lit a fire in the barbecue and puffed smoke
in at the back of the molehill.

15

Mole got busy at once. Hooks were required, and screens and pipes—and some vents. Very quickly he was able to install a smokehouse behind his kitchen. Smoked worms were Mole's favorite supper!

17

That summer Mole dug the strawberry plot very
thoroughly. Mr. Carrington spoke to a local farmer
who had heard that moles dislike loud music.

18

Mr. Carrington buried loudspeakers, amplifiers and other sound equipment near Mole's home.

There was music everywhere! Mole was very happy.

Sometimes he played along on his
cornet during the long summer evenings.

21

Mole used every corner of the garden to demonstrate his talents as a digger. Eventually Mr. Carrington came to rely on him completely. He would relax with his family, trusting that Mole would do a quality job in the garden.

By autumn, Mr. Carrington could not think of
anything else to do for Mole. There was not much to
be done in the garden, and there didn't seem to be
enough room in the house anymore. So the
Carringtons decided to move.

The whole family began to look for a new house.
When Mr. Carrington said, "This is the place!"
Mole was just as excited as the rest of the family.

It was a good, big house, surrounded by lawns.
Mr. Carrington could imagine a vegetable patch
at the back. So could Mole.

It takes a lot of hard work to move. Everything must be carefully packed before the furniture and boxes are loaded into the moving van. There was work for everyone.

Mole didn't have a moment to spare as he scurried from molehill to van with piles of his belongings. Imagine his horror as he brought up the last load to discover that his family had forgotten him!

Bounding onto his bicycle, Mole tore off after the
van. Before long he caught sight of it ahead, waiting
in a traffic jam. With a whoop of joy, Mole overtook
the tractors, cars and trucks waiting at the busy
intersection. He overtook the moving van and
streaked ahead, down the road to his new home.

Mole took one look at the smooth green lawn. It was clear Mr. Carrington was going to need a great deal of help. There was no time to lose.

When the Carringtons arrived a few minutes later, they were just in time to see Mole finishing his first molehill in the new garden.

Mole was pleased.

He could tell that Mr. Carrington was surprised.